IDAA TRAIL

Idaa Trail

IN THE STEPS OF OUR ANCESTORS

WENDY STEPHENSON

PICTURES BY
AUTUMN DOWNEY

BASED ON THE
ARCHEOLOGICAL RESEARCH OF
Tom Andrews, John B. Zoe AND Harry Simpson,
AND THE ORAL TRADITION OF
THE Dogrib, OR Tłįchǫ, people

GROUNDWOOD BOOKS
HOUSE OF ANANSI PRESS
TORONTO BERKELEY

Groundwood Books / House of Anansi Press
110 Spadina Avenue, Suite 801, Toronto, Ontario M5V 2K4

Distributed in the USA by Publishers Group West
1700 Fourth Street, Berkeley, CA 94710

We acknowledge for their financial support of our publishing
program the Canada Council for the Arts, the Government of
Canada through the Book Publishing Industry Development
Program (BPIDP) and the Ontario Arts Council.

ONTARIO ARTS COUNCIL
CONSEIL DES ARTS DE L'ONTARIO

Library and Archives Canada Cataloging in Publication
Stephenson, Wendy
Idaa Trail: in the steps of our ancestors / Wendy Stephenson;
pictures by Autumn Downey.
ISBN-13: 978-0-88899-576-6
ISBN-10: 0-88899-576-8
1. Dogrib Indians–Juvenile literature. 2. Idaa Trail
(N.W.T.)–Juvenile literature. 3. Northwest Territories–Description
and travel–Juvenile literature. I. Downey, Autumn. II. Title.
E99.T4S73 2005   j971.9'3004972   C2004-906051-1

Design by Michael Solomon
Printed and bound in China

To this and future generations of Dogrib youth

CONTENTS

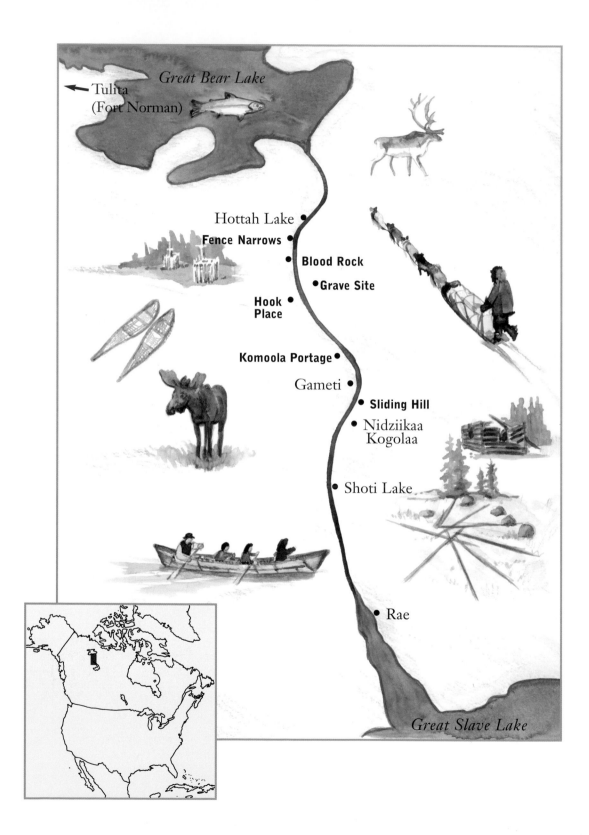

Great Bear Lake

← Tulita
(Fort Norman)

Hottah Lake •
Fence Narrows •
Blood Rock •
•**Grave Site**
**Hook
Place** •

Komoola Portage •
Gameti •
• **Sliding Hill**
• Nidziikaa
Kogolaa
• Shoti Lake

• Rae

Great Slave Lake

Chapter One
GETTING READY FOR THE TRIP

JUNE 28 and sixth grade was finally over. John's cousins had called him a few weeks ago to see if he could go on a canoe trip with their grandparents. He was excited but a little bit scared, too. This canoe trip was going to be at least four weeks long. They planned to paddle all the way from Rae to Hottah Lake on an old canoe route called the Idaa Trail.

"People used the trail for hundreds of years to get from Fort Rae to Fort Norman," explained his mom. "They traveled by dog team in winter and birchbark canoe in summer. Your grandparents used to travel on that trail with their families when they were your age. Now they want to show you and your cousins the important places on the way."

The next week John's parents drove him from Yellowknife to Rae where his cousins, Nora and Peter, and his grandparents, Etseh and Etsi, were getting ready for the trip.

"John! Come and look at the map," Peter called as soon as he saw his cousin.

They gathered around the kitchen table. Their grandfather slowly traced a route that would take them along rivers, lakes and portages, north to Hottah Lake. It was a route that had been traveled by many generations of Dogrib people.

Etsi smiled at the excitement in the eyes of her three grandchildren.

They spent the next day packing. Two large packs, one smaller pack and one tent would go in each canoe.

"*Ts'ekoa*, pass me the sugar," Etsi asked Nora.

Into the food pack went tea, flour, oatmeal, raisins, sugar, lard, baking powder, dried caribou meat, rice, salt and a freshly baked bannock. Then Etsi packed her sewing kit, a few pots and some dishes.

Etseh carefully placed the guns in their caribou-hide cases and checked his ax and fish net.

"We can't forget the teapot," laughed Etsi.

"Or the bug jackets," said Nora.

"What about the bush radio?" asked Peter.

"*He?e*," replied Etseh. He shoved the bright orange radio into the pack.

That night John lay on the couch and tried to fall asleep. But he kept imagining what lay ahead. Fishing, swimming,

campfires. Bugs, bad weather, bears? He tossed and turned then finally fell asleep to the rhythm of his grandfather's snoring.

"*Ho!* Time to get up," called Etseh. "No use sleeping till noon today! We need to pack the canoes and get going. The weather's good and the water's calm."

The three cousins followed the smell of sizzling bacon and eggs to the kitchen.

"Eat up! These will be your last eggs for a while," teased Etsi.

Later that morning, as they finished loading the canoes, friends and relatives came down to the dock. Even the chief came to see them off. He said a prayer and made an offering of

tobacco to the water for a safe trip. Everyone waved and wished them good luck as they paddled away.

John, sitting in the middle of his grandfather's canoe, began paddling quickly.

"Slow down, John! You won't have any strength left if you keep paddling like that," laughed Etseh.

Nora turned around and laughed, too. She was just two years older than John, but she had been on trips with her grandparents before. Peter, the oldest cousin, paddled the canoe behind them while joking with his grandmother about eating too much breakfast.

Chapter Two
SHOTI LAKE

THE FIRST days of the trip were long and hot as they paddled on the lakes and rivers north of Rae. At the end of each day Nora's arms ached and Peter's knees were stiff. John was so hungry he thought he could eat a moose. On the fourth day they reached the portage before Shoti Lake.

"We'll camp here," their grandfather told them.

They pulled the canoes up on shore and unloaded them. John groaned every time he lifted one of the heavy packs.

"By the end of this trip, we won't hear any more of those sounds from you," said Etseh. "You'll be a lot stronger."

After emptying the canoes, the cousins scrambled over the rocks to explore the site. Etsi walked quietly along the shore. She seemed to be looking for something.

"What are you doing, Etsi?" asked Peter.

"Here it is!" his grandmother said. She bent down beside some old curled pieces of birchbark. "I remember coming to this place when I was about your age. It was fall time, and our whole family was traveling north in birchbark canoes to spend the winter trapping. One of our canoes had a tear in it. We took some birchbark from that tree over there to fix it."

The cousins could see a tree with a huge black scar where the bark had been carefully peeled away. Even so, the tree was still alive.

"But then it started to get cold," Etsi continued. "The lake began to freeze. We decided to leave our canoes here for the

winter. We waited for enough snow to fall and then continued on by dog team." She pointed to some pieces of bark and wood lying by her feet. "What do you think these are?"

Peter studied the sun-bleached wood and rotting birch bark. He looked up at his grandmother, smiling. "Canoes! These are the two you left behind."

Etsi nodded, "That was about sixty years ago."

"Let's take some of the pieces home with us," said John.

"*Ile.* We must protect our history. Leave them here for others to see," replied his grandmother.

"Tell us more stories about birchbark canoes," asked Nora. "They must have been tippy! How long did it take to make one?"

"Let's set up the radio first," said Etseh. He and Etsi liked to listen to people chatting on the bush channel. "Then we can get the tents ready and have something to eat. We can tell stories after that."

Etseh and Nora strung the long antenna for the radio between two trees while the others put up the tents. After a big meal of soup and bannock, John lay by the fire with his eyes closed, listening to his grandmother.

"We made canoes in the springtime," explained Etsi. "A large family would make two canoes, sometimes more. The men cut the wood and everyone helped gather the spruce gum, spruce roots and birchbark. When we took bark from the tree we never cut too deeply. That way the tree would stay alive.

Then the women sewed the bark pieces together with split spruce roots."

Etsi made a cut on the trunk of a smooth birch tree and carefully peeled away a small piece of bark. She made a few folds and in minutes had a small birchbark cup in her hand. She looked at Nora.

"*Dzon, ts'ekoa.* This is for you," she said.

"We heated the spruce gum and put it on the seams of the birchbark canoes," Etsi continued. "Once it was cool and hard, it kept the canoes from leaking. We carved our own paddles, too."

Etsi stopped and looked over at John. He had fallen asleep.

"That's enough for now," Etseh said quietly. "Let's get some sleep. It has been a good long day. *Masi.*"

Chapter Three
VILLAGE BESIDE NIDZII

EARLY THE NEXT morning, Etseh nudged Peter from his sleeping bag.

"Come and help me set the fish net," he said.

They went down to the canoe without waking the others. Before pushing off from shore, Etseh carefully laid a branch from a cranberry bush on the water. "I will be thankful for some fresh fish!" he said softly.

It didn't take long to put the net in the water. Within an hour they were paddling back to camp. As they got closer, Etseh spotted John struggling to start a fire. He chuckled to himself as they brought the canoe up on shore.

"I've watched Etseh make a fire every day!" thought John. "How come this one won't light?"

He was about to give up when Etseh walked over with an armful of dry spruce twigs. Without a word, he lifted the

big pieces of wood that John had been fussing over and placed the dry twigs underneath them.

"Now try," he said.

In a few minutes tea was bubbling over a blazing fire.

"You know, to us the land is like a book," Etseh told his grandchildren as they ate breakfast. "Each place has a name and a story. After we check the net and dry the fish, we'll go to a place called Nidziikaa Kogolaa. There are some good stories and some very sad stories about that old village."

"What happened there? Tell us!" urged Nora.

"Be patient," said her grandmother. "You must see each place before we tell you the stories. Finish your food and then we'll check the net and pack up."

The net was full. Soon a dozen fat whitefish lay on a blanket of freshly cut willows. Nora and John helped Etsi cut the fish and hang them to dry. This way they could take the fish with them to eat later. Lunch was a yummy fish soup.

"We'll paddle to Nidziikaa Kogolaa when you're finished," said Etseh.

Nora and John were eager to see the village and hear the stories their grandfather had promised them.

It was mid-afternoon when the group pulled their canoes up onto a rocky shore. Etseh and Etsi led the way along a well-worn path through some willows.

"I can see something," called Peter. "It looks like an old chimney."

As they came into a clearing, they saw several tall stone chimneys and a few old cabins.

"What was this place?" asked John.

Etseh sat down on the grass and began his story.

"Long before the treaty of 1921 our people came to this place. Those chimneys are from cabins built more than one hundred years ago. People lived here all winter and part of the summer. They taught their children the ways of the bush: how to choose good fishing spots, how to make things from wood — like canoes and toboggans.

"A man named K'aawidaa had a cabin here. He was an important trading chief for our people, the Dogrib. He took furs to Rae to trade and came back bringing huge bundles of supplies."

"What kinds of things would he bring back?" asked John.

"Flour, tea, knives, traps, axes, cloth, guns, tobacco," explained Etsi. "Even fancy boots like these!" She laughed as she pointed to an old pair of black lace-up boots partly buried in the ground.

"People must have been pretty happy when he returned with all that stuff!" said John.

Nora had wandered over behind one of the cabins. "Oh, look! There are graves over here," she called to the others.

Standing by the graves, Etseh told the story of how a flu

epidemic had spread through that part of the country back in 1928. Hundreds of people died, and at Nidziikaa Kogolaa, at least twenty lost their lives. After that no one wanted to live there anymore, so they abandoned the village.

The grandparents knelt beside the graves and prayed for the people buried there.

Then Etseh said, "Let's fix up these graves a bit. Take those bushes away from that grave over there, John and Nora. Straighten those boards, Peter. *Nezi.*"

"I'm getting hot!" grumbled John when they had finished. "How about a swim?"

"*He?e,*" said Etseh. "It has been a long day. Let's paddle to that island over there. We'll make camp and then you can swim."

"But why can't we camp here?" whined John. "I'm too tired to paddle anymore."

"If we camp on that island, we'll have a nice breeze to keep the bugs away," explained Etseh. "There shouldn't be any bears, either."

"Okay, let's go!" agreed John.

Chapter Four
SLIDING HILL

THEY SPENT the next few days camping on different islands and paddling across several small lakes. The mosquitoes and horseflies started to get bad. John was grumpy, even with his bug jacket on.

"Etseh, I can't stand these bugs. What did people do in the old days?"

Etseh smiled. "Whenever we camped we would make a smoky fire to keep the bugs away. We also had a lot of patience.

By the way, it would be a good idea if you and Nora didn't use so much of that smelly soap and shampoo. The better you smell, the more the bugs love you," he said.

"Time to make camp," Etseh shouted to the others in the blue canoe. "We can stop here, and I'll show you Hodoodzoo, the Sliding Hill."

Nora and John made a fire while the others got some food ready. Peter took the dry fish out of a pack, and Etseh reached for a golden bannock made that morning.

Etsi went to the lake to get water for tea. "In the old days, if we didn't have tea, we took the inside bark of a spruce tree and boiled it," she explained, walking up from the lake. "We boiled the fish we caught and drank that water, too, to get vitamins. My grandparents told me they used birchbark to make pails and put spruce gum on the seams to stop them from leaking. Just like the canoes. Long, long ago, they cooked food in birchbark pots by heating rocks in the fire and placing them in the pots full of water. The water would heat up enough to cook the meat or fish."

"Things are pretty easy these days!" laughed John, holding the metal teapot.

After lunch everyone walked toward the Sliding Hill.

"Since long before the white people came, this place has been called Hodoodzoo because of the legend of Yamozhah and the giant wolverine," Etseh explained.

"The giant wolverine used to trick people into sliding down this hill. He placed sharp stakes at the bottom that would kill them.

"The people were frightened so they asked Yamozhah for help. He tricked the giant wolverine by pretending to lie dead on the stakes at the bottom of the hill. The giant wolverine found him there and dragged him back to camp. He was just about to cook Yamozhah and eat him, when Yamozhah jumped up, grabbed a stick and killed the giant wolverine. The wolverine's small pups quickly climbed up the trunk of a spruce tree.

"'Please don't kill us,' they cried. Their tears ran down the trunk of the spruce. 'If you spare our lives we'll give you a gift. We'll turn our tears into spruce gum. You and your people can use it for waterproofing the seams of your birchbark canoes, for medicine and all sorts of things.'

"Yamozhah agreed, as long as the wolverines promised never to become giants again. That is why you see spruce gum on the trees today.

"Nobody passes by this place without stopping," their grandfather continued. "In the past, people came here to slide in the summer and winter. They used this hill to predict the future. People slid down the hill on the tip of a spruce tree. If they went straight down to the bottom without spinning around then it was said they would live a long life. If they spun around halfway down the hill then they would not live to see their gray hairs because the land was not happy with them. That's the story of this place."

Minutes later the three cousins stood at the top of the hill looking at the places where the crusty black lichen had been worn away from the rock after many years of sliding.

"Is it our turn now?" yelled Nora, sitting on her spruce branch.

"Go ahead!" shouted Etsi.

One by one, the three cousins slid straight down the hill.

"You're lucky!" said Etsi. "I guess you will live to see your gray hairs."

As they walked back to the canoes, Etsi noticed Peter rubbing his hand.

"What happened?" she asked.

"I guess I scraped myself when I slid down the hill," said Peter. "It doesn't really hurt."

Etsi looked at the cut then took out her knife and carefully peeled some soft gum off the trunk of a nearby spruce tree.

"Put this on your cut. It will heal quickly," she said.

The past few days had been hot and sunny, but now the

weather was changing. The wind was stronger, and John noticed Etseh watching some large dark clouds to the west.

"This weather isn't looking good," he said. "I think we should camp on that island by the point. We can wait there and see what happens."

The canoes changed direction and headed toward the island. Suddenly, a gust of wind blew across the lake. The waves rose and water splashed into the canoe. John grabbed the sides.

"Pick up your paddle, John!" yelled Etseh. "We need every-one to paddle hard."

Minutes later they struggled to pull the canoes up on the shore of the island. They could hear low rumbles of thunder in the distance.

"Let's get the tents up before it rains!" called Peter. Scurrying around, they put the packs under the canoes and set up the tents.

"Come into our tent for now. It's bigger," called Etseh.

"And bring the chocolate bars!" added John.

Sitting close together inside the tent, they listened to slow drips of rain falling overhead. Soon the dripping turned into a downpour.

"That was good timing," said John. "We would have been soaked out there! Does anyone have the chocolate bars?"

Etsi smiled and dug around in her food pack. "*Dawhidi!* Here, chew on this dry meat. It will keep you from feeling hungry."

"Hmmm," mumbled John, "not quite what I was hoping for."

"If we move those packs a bit, we can play hand games," said Etseh. He reached outside the tent for some small sticks. "First we need two teams. Each team sits in a row, facing the

other. Then a person from one team has to guess which person on the other team is holding this rifle shell. You need to try to trick the other team so they can't guess whose hand it's in. These sticks in the middle will be our counters to see which team wins."

During the hand games, Etseh played a drum using a stick and the cover of the bush radio.

After a while the cousins began to yawn. It was time for bed.

Chapter Five
KOMOOLA PORTAGE

THE WIND blew for two more days. On the third day it was quiet. Etseh and Etsi sat by the fire sipping cold tea and listening to the bush radio. They could hear voices chatting and laughing from Gameti, Whati and Kugluktuk. Muffled snores came from the grandchildren's tent.

"We have a long paddle across the lake today. I'm glad the wind has died down," said Etsi.

"*He?e.* We'll be passing by Gameti, too," replied Etseh. "At the end of that lake is the portage at Komoola. We should get going."

Etsi went to waken the grandchildren.

They had oatmeal, dry fish and tea for breakfast and then loaded the two canoes. Before getting in, Etseh asked each grandchild to take two thin branches from a birch tree and twist them together to make a circle.

"This will be our offering today," he explained as they placed them gently in the water. "We want to have a safe crossing of this big lake. *Masi,*" he prayed.

By the middle of the day they could see the houses of Gameti.

"It's time to say hello!" said Etseh.

The sound of three gunshots at the back of the canoe was deafening.

"What are you doing?" asked John, holding his hands over his ears.

"Pretty soon we'll be at Gameti. This is how we tell them we're on our way," explained Etseh, his gun in the air.

They heard the sound of answering gunshots. John could hardly wait to get to Gameti to buy the chocolate bar he had been dreaming of!

Within minutes they were having tea with some of their relatives. They exchanged stories for a while and then continued on their way. (Only after Nora and John made a quick trip to the store with a five-dollar bill from their grandfather!)

"I wish we could have stayed longer," said John.

"Maybe I could have even had a shower," agreed Nora.

"I know," said Etseh. "But today the weather's good and we need to keep traveling if we are going to make it to Hottah Lake by the end of next week."

They continued paddling down the large lake, staying close to shore in case the wind came up again.

"That was a long paddle," said Nora, pausing to rub her shoulder as they approached the end of the lake.

"I'll be glad to stretch my legs," said John. "Is this where we're going to camp?"

"*Ile*," replied Etseh. "This is Komoola portage. We can make camp after we get to the other side. Better get your muscles ready!"

Etsi reached into her food bag and got out the last of her dried meat. They each had a piece along with a cup of clear, cold water from the lake.

"I'm getting tired of fish and dried meat," thought John. "I wish I had some chips or a can of pop."

"*Sehkw'on!*" said Etseh. "When you carry your pack, it's

important to have it well balanced on your back. Etsi, remember the story of that woman? She was walking over a rocky portage. Her pack was not on properly, and she fell to her death over a cliff."

Etsi nodded.

The grandparents helped Nora, John and Peter adjust their packs and got ready to lead the way over the portage.

"We'll take packs on this trip and leave the canoes and paddles for the next time across," said Etseh, starting off along the path with his big pack and gun. "Don't wander off. You could get hurt or lost. Stay together and follow the trail."

Peter, at the back of the group, was anxious to get to the other side of the portage and take the heavy pack off his back. He was carrying his shotgun in one hand and was feeling impatient. He didn't seem to be listening to his grandfather.

They continued along the trail, going down into a low, wet area where someone had laid poles on the path to walk across. John wondered when they would ever get to the other end of the portage. After about an hour, they came to a clearing at the edge of the next lake. John flopped his pack on the ground.

"Phew! Only one more trip. Hey, where's Peter?"

Etseh and Etsi looked at each other with worried eyes.

"Maybe he just stopped to tie his shoe," said Nora hopefully.

Etseh told everyone to wait. He took his gun and headed back along the trail. Nora and John, happy to take a break, sat on the flat rocks, resting their backs against their packs.

It wasn't long before Etseh and Peter appeared. Peter was soaked up to his knees and looked a little embarrassed.

"What happened?" asked John, trying not to laugh.

Peter told them how he had decided to take a shortcut and ended up walking through a swamp. Then he had heard Etseh calling.

"Weren't you scared?" asked Nora.

"Kind of. I thought I knew where I was," Peter said, grinning sheepishly at his grandparents.

On the last trip back across the portage Etseh and Peter carried the canoes while the others brought the last of the gear.

"I'm wearing my bug jacket," said Peter. "There'll be millions of bugs under this canoe. Yech." Off they went, Peter's wet shoes making squishy noises as he walked.

John and Nora caught up to the others at the end of the portage. They could see Etseh and Peter crouched by the shore behind some tall bulrushes. Peter had his gun ready.

John and Nora snuck up beside them. Etseh pointed at the water.

Swimming in and out of the tall grass were four ducks. John's mouth began to water at the thought of fresh meat for supper.

Within a couple of hours, they were all sitting around the fire, fresh duck roasting on the grill in front of them.

Chapter Six
HOOK PLACE

JOHN CLIMBED out of the tent the next morning and stretched. The sun warmed his bare arms. The loons called from the lake. And there were hardly any bugs! It was a perfect morning for a short walk along the shore.

To his surprise he found a low wooden structure partly hidden in the bush. Curious, he moved the branches covering it and looked more closely. He could tell it was old.

"Maybe it's some kind of trap," he thought.

At breakfast John told the others what he had seen.

"You found a *dechi*, a fish cache," said Etseh. "People used

to come here in the fall time. They set their nets over there and caught lots of whitefish," he explained, pointing along the shore. "They stuck branches in their tails and made *Kligotse*, or stickfish. Then they hung the fish inside the cache. The cache was covered with heavy logs and rocks so bears, foxes or wolverines couldn't get in. In the winter, when people passed by here again with their dog teams, they had lots of fish to feed them."

"Sounds like a lot of work," said Peter.

After they inspected the old fish cache, they took down their tents and loaded the canoes.

"The food pack is getting lighter!" said John.

"That's because we're running out of food," sighed Nora.

It was mid-afternoon when Etseh steered the canoe toward a narrow spot between two islands. Nora and John stopped

dling. The water was so clear and blue that it was like looking through glass.

"Wow! Look at all those neat rocks," John exclaimed.

"Hey," said Nora, "I just saw a fish swim by."

"We need to catch our supper," said Etseh. "This is another place where people have caught fish for years and years. We've always needed fish to feed our dogs and ourselves."

"I like the old ways, but I can catch a fish for supper with my new fishing rod," said John, climbing out of the canoe.

"Wait for me!" called Nora.

John cast his line out over and over while Nora looked for the perfect lure in her tackle box. Peter and Etsi sat on a rock watching.

"I caught one! It's huge!" called John, struggling with his bending rod. Peter ran over to help him land the fish. It was a big, fat lake trout.

"This will feed all of us for sure," John said proudly. "It must be a fifteen pounder!"

Etsi grinned as she looked at the trout lying on the grass. She took the fish by its gills and showed Nora and Peter the best way to clean it.

"This is a good fishing spot," said Etsi. "It's called Dahʔak'e, or Hook Place. In the old days, people would tie two lines to a spruce branch. They would attach a hook to one line, and they would use the other to secure the branch to shore. When the branch was thrown onto the water, the hook and line would dangle below the surface, attracting the fish. If the branch bobbed in the water, a fish was on the hook."

"But what did they use for hooks and line?" asked John.

"They didn't have this kind of fishhook," said Etsi, pointing to John's yellow and red lure. "They used to take the two upper

teeth from a muskrat or beaver and split them in two. For fishing line, they used willow bark and twisted it like sinew. They could also tie the willow line and muskrat-tooth hook to the end of a long pole. That's how we used to catch fish! Pretty smart, eh?"

John and his grandmother made a fire on the rocky shore. They couldn't wait until supper time to cook John's fresh lake trout. Nora sat on a nearby rock, feet dangling in the water. She watched Peter and her grandfather as they took turns fishing. It wasn't long before they were cleaning two more fish.

"*Nezi,*" said Etseh, scooping a drink of the clear, cold water with his hands. "We have lots to eat. Now let's try that lake trout. I'm hungry!"

They ate in silence, enjoying the delicious fish and watching loons play near the shore.

"Can we camp here and play more hand games tonight?" asked Nora. "I love this island."

"It is pretty here, *ts'ekoa*," said Etsi. "But there's no place to put our tents."

"Let's paddle down the lake," said Etseh. "There's a good camping place not too far away."

Paddling along the shore of the mainland, Nora could see something on the top of a hill in the distance.

"Etseh, what's that?" she asked.

Etseh waited for the other canoe to catch up. "That's the grave of Madelaine. She married K'aawidaa's nephew, Kwajii, and was buried there in 1941. Do you remember K'aawidaa, the trading chief who had a cabin at Nidziikaa Kogolaa?"

"I remember," said John. "He used to bring back all that neat trading stuff for the people there."

"*He?e*," nodded Etsi.

"What's Madelaine's story?" asked Nora.

"First we'll go and pay her a visit," said Etseh. "She asked to be buried up there because it's a place where people could always visit her — by canoe in the summer or by dog team in the winter."

"Wow. She sounds popular," said Nora.

They climbed the hill through the charred remains of an old forest fire and admired the view from the grave.

"You can see in all directions!" said John with his arms stretched wide.

The white fence around Madelaine's grave stood out among bright pink fireweed.

"Madelaine was a powerful woman," began Etsi. "People said she had strong medicine. Before she died, she told people to visit her here. She told them to leave her something, and if there was anything they wanted to ask for it."

John looked over at Etseh. He had placed some bullets and matches beside the cross. He seemed to be talking to Madelaine. Everyone helped pull out the weeds and clear away the overgrown bushes around her grave.

Back in the canoe, John turned to look at his grandfather. "Etseh, did you ask for anything at Madelaine's grave?"

"We haven't had any meat for many days now," replied Etseh. "I asked her for a moose."

Chapter Seven
BLOOD ROCK

TWO GUNSHOTS made John jump out of his sleeping bag. They sounded close! He grabbed his hat, pulled on his socks and shoes and quickly unzipped the tent. Peter was already outside.

"Where's Etseh?" John asked.

"The shots came from over there," said Peter.

"Let's go!"

They found Etseh at the edge of a grassy swamp. He was busy with his hunting knife, bending over the large dark-brown shape of a moose.

"Wow! It's huge," whispered John. "Madelaine must be happy we visited her. You got what you asked for, Etseh!"

"*Heʔe*," said Etseh. "Now the work begins. Go back to camp, tell the others and bring back some knives with you."

When they returned, John noticed two moose ears stuck on top of a tall willow bush.

"What did you do that for?" he asked Etseh.

"We always do that. It's good luck for hunting. That way the moose won't hear the hunter next time," explained Etseh. "We also make sure we thank the moose for giving itself to us."

They spent many hours skinning the moose. Once Etseh had cut away the hide, they had to cut the dark red meat from the animal and carry it all back to camp. John couldn't believe how much work it was.

Then Etsi and Nora sat on a bed of spruce boughs cutting the meat into long thin strips for drying. Peter, John and Etseh built a rack where they could hang the huge moose hide.

"Now we need to take all the hair off the hide and hang it to dry. That way it will be lighter to carry," said Etseh. "It's hard work so we'll take turns scraping."

Later in the day they all sat by the fire munching on moose meat. Etsi had cooked the bones well so that any leftover meat fell off easily. After the meal the bones would be carefully piled up and left at the edge of the camp.

"What happens if a bear smells all this meat?" John asked between bites.

"That's why we camped on an island. We have a gun, too. But remember, if you ever see a bear, you must talk to it. My parents always told us that you should talk softly to bears, telling them who you are and why you are there. If you do this, the bear won't bother you."

That night John lay in his sleeping bag thinking of all they had done that day. He couldn't wait to tell his parents. Then he thought of his grandfather's bear story. Every sound outside the tent made his eyes pop open. Finally, sleep took over.

They spent three days at Moose Camp, as John called it. This gave them enough time to finish drying the meat and big moose hide.

Etseh took the hide off the rack and rolled it into a neat bundle. "John! *Dzonchleh!* Try carrying this now," he said.

John stood still as Etseh placed the bundle on his back and put the tumpline over his forehead.

"Hey, this isn't bad at all! I thought it would be really heavy," John said.

They packed the hide in the canoe along with all their gear, gave thanks to the water and pushed off.

"Where are we going today?" asked Nora.

"See that big flat hill up ahead?" said Etseh. "We call that Kwe?ehdoo, or Blood Rock. We'll stop there, and I'll tell you another story about Yamozhah."

When they reached the shore, Nora hopped out of the canoe and grabbed the rope. Soon both canoes were tied up, and they started climbing the hill. Luckily a cool breeze kept the bugs away.

"Why is it so flat up here?" asked John.

Resting on a large rock, Etseh explained. "This hill is where Yamozhah was born, along with his mischievous brother Ts'idzoo. The story is that this hill is really the skull of Yamozhah's giant grandfather. They say that the brothers killed their grandfather by cutting open the top of his skull when he was sleeping. They threw hot rocks into his head, and he turned to stone."

The cousins wandered over the bald crown of the hill, imagining they were walking on a giant's skull. Etseh and Etsi waved them back for the rest of the story.

"Look, you can see a big crack here. Whenever people come to this place they kneel on this rock."

John looked down at the rock. It had been worn smooth by people kneeling on it over the years.

"People say a prayer here and leave tobacco or matches for the old grandfather," said Etsi. "Then they drop a stone down the crack. If they hear it drop to the bottom, it means they will live a long time. If they don't hear a sound, it means they won't have a long life."

Etseh reached into a small pouch and placed a pinch of tobacco in a tiny crack, murmuring a few words. Then Nora dropped a stone into the crack and listened carefully.

"It hit water!" she said.

John went next. He, too, heard that lucky sound from down below.

On the way back to the canoes, Etseh stopped by a pile of rocks.

"Look at how these rocks have been broken. This is another special place. These rocks were used long ago for making stone tools."

"You mean spear points and arrowheads?" asked Peter.

"*He?e*," nodded Etseh.

Peter looked around, hoping to find an old arrowhead.

"It's getting late," said Etsi.

"And I'm hungry!" said John.

"Can we play hand games again tonight?" asked Nora.

"Let's paddle to that point over there and set up camp. We can play hand games after we eat," Etseh said, untying the canoe.

"But what about bears?" John asked. "I thought we were supposed to camp on islands!"

"There are no islands at this end of the lake," replied Etseh. *"Asanile."*

That night after a good meal of roasted moose and rice, and some hand games, Peter and John lay in their tent talking about Yamozhah and the giant grandfather. Peter fell asleep thinking of the days when people hunted caribou and moose with bows and stone-tipped arrows.

But John lay awake for a long time, listening for the sound of bears.

Chapter Eight
FENCE NARROWS

"WHAT ARE you looking at, Etseh?" asked John as he scrambled out of his tent the next morning.

"*Sah k'e.*"

"Bear tracks?" asked John.

"*He?e,*" said Etseh. "Looks like we had a visitor last night. He didn't bother anything."

John bent down to take a closer look at the tracks. He had never seen such big paw prints! "I'm glad we're moving camp today," he thought.

"We only have a few days left before we get picked up at

Hottah Lake," Etseh told the cousins as they ate dried fish and bannock for breakfast.

"Can't we keep going?" asked John. "We could use the radio and tell the plane to come next week instead."

"I thought you really wanted some chips and another chocolate bar!" laughed Etsi.

"Not anymore," announced John. "All this meat and fish tastes pretty good."

They paddled through morning rain showers and by midday the sun peeked through the clouds.

"Today we'll camp by Kweikaa, or Fence Narrows," said Etseh. "Let's pull into shore over there," he said, pointing with his paddle.

They paddled to the place where the lake grew narrow, hugged between two hilly shorelines, and pulled both canoes on shore.

The grandparents watched proudly as their three grandchildren set up camp. "They have learned well," said Etsi to her husband.

"*Nezi*," nodded Etseh.

Once all the work was finished, Nora, Peter and John took a quick dip in the lake.

"*Dzonchleh*. Let's take a walk over this way," pointed Etseh. "I want to show you something."

Suddenly a piece of wood under a bush caught Etseh's attention. Smiling, he picked it up.

"That looks like an old toy airplane," said John.

"*He?e*. I can remember camping here with my family a long time ago. My grandfather used to make toys for us. This was one of my favorites," he said as he gently placed it back under the bush.

"Aren't you going to take it home?" asked Nora.

"*Ile*. If I leave it here, I can come and visit it another time," said Etseh.

They walked on to a clearing. Peter bent down and picked up a piece of stone.

John ran over. "What did you find?"

"I don't know for sure, but it looks like an arrowhead!" said Peter. He handed the stone to his grandfather.

"*He?e*," Etseh nodded as he gently placed the sharpened stone where Peter had found it. "A long time ago, when it was spring and the caribou were going back to the barrenlands, this is the place where our people would make a tree fence on the lake ice. They would camp on this side of the lake. Then they would cut down trees. It was hard work to cut so many. Down

on the ice they lined the trees up side by side to make a long fence like this." Etseh took a stick and started to draw a picture in the sand.

"The hunters waited at the end of the fence all night long. They sent the children to the top of that hill over there to look out for the caribou," said Etseh as he pointed across the narrow stretch of lake. "When they saw the caribou coming, the children signaled to the hunters below. The hunters hid behind rocks at the end of the fence, waiting to ambush the caribou as they came down the lake. That's how our people caught so many caribou. All that's left now are rocks from the campfires and the tipi rings and the odd spear point or arrowhead like the one you found, Peter."

"That sounds like a good way to catch a lot of caribou," said John.

"*He?e*," said Etsi. "They also tied pieces of cloth to some of the trees to scare the caribou. It helped keep them inside the fence. And they set snares between the trees to catch some of the animals."

"Why did they have to kill so many?" asked Nora.

"Without caribou, our people could not survive," explained Etseh. "We needed caribou for many things. Food from their meat, tools from their antlers and bones, clothing and tipis from their hides. After a big hunt like the one at the caribou fence, everyone worked together to cut meat and scrape hides."

Etsi had walked over to a flat area. She was looking at a large circle of stones and long gray poles partly buried in the lichen.

"What did you find?" Peter asked.

"This is a place where people used to put their caribou-skin tipis," said Etsi.

"This must have been a big tipi!" exclaimed Peter as he looked around the circle.

"Some tipis could hold more than one family. It took about thirty caribou skins to make a tipi this big," said Etsi.

"Now I know why they had to hunt so many!" said Nora.

"Do you remember the story about the family that got their first canvas tent?" Etseh asked his wife.

"*He?e!* That's a good story," said Etsi.

"A long time ago, this family went to the trading post with their furs and came home with their first canvas-wall tent," began Etseh. "When they got back to camp, they spread the square tent on the ground. They had never seen that kind of tent before. They were used to caribou-skin tipis. Around and around the tent they walked, trying to figure out how to put it up. For a few days people talked about the tent, wondering how it was supposed to work. Finally the women took out their knives and cut it up and made a canvas tipi — just like the caribou-hide tipis they were used to!"

"Now everyone uses canvas tents or light camping tents when they go in the bush. No more caribou-skin tipis," said Etsi.

"Speaking of tents, it looks like rain again," said Nora.

"Let's go back to camp and have supper before we get soaked," said Etseh.

Chapter Nine
ARRIVING AT HOTTAH LAKE

The next day after a short portage and a few hours of paddling they reached Hottah Lake.

"This is where we get picked up!" said Nora.

"*He?e*," replied Etseh. "Now we need to go to that island so we can radio the plane and tell them exactly where we are. We'll see if they can come tomorrow."

They arrived at the island around noon, set up camp and strung the radio antenna along a high rocky hill. The three grandchildren set off to swim in the lake.

"Make sure you check the water before you jump in. There could be sharp rocks!" warned Etsi.

"Okay," called John. "The water's so cold we won't be in for long!"

While Etsi watched the grandchildren, Etseh climbed the hill to use the radio. A short while later, he was back.

"The plane will be here at one o'clock tomorrow," he said.

Etseh got the map out after supper and showed his grandchildren where the Idaa Trail went after Hottah Lake.

"We're camped here," he said pointing to their island. "In the old days people used to go to the end of Hottah Lake, paddle down this river, go along the shore of Great Bear Lake and then portage past Grizzly Bear Mountain. That portage took many days."

"Why would people want to go that far?" asked Peter.

"They were on their way to Fort Norman to trade," replied Etsi.

"That's a long way to go shopping," said John.

"You're right," said Etsi, chuckling. "And then when they did get to Great Bear Lake, they had to be very careful of the wind. The waves can be huge on that lake."

"Once they finished their trading, did they portage and paddle all the way back to Rae on the Idaa Trail?" asked Nora.

"*He?e,*" replied Etseh. John and Nora looked at each other with wide eyes imagining what a long trip that must have been.

The next day John woke up to the sound of rain tapping on the tent. "Uh, oh. Maybe the plane won't land if the weather's bad," he thought. He poked his head outside. His grandparents were spreading a tarp between some trees.

"Come and help us, John," said Etseh. "We can stand under here and keep our gear dry until the plane comes."

"Do you think it can land in this weather?" asked John.

"*He?e.* The clouds are still high and the pilot can see us even though it's raining a bit," said Etseh. "We'll call them on the radio in a few hours to give them a weather report."

They took down the tents for the last time and piled their gear under the canoes and tarp to keep dry.

"Tell us a story about this part of the lake," asked Nora as they sat around the fire under the tarp.

"This lake is also called Intse Ti, which means Moose Lake in Slavey," explained Etseh. "Not far from here is a place where the Sahtu Dene and Dogrib people would meet once a year."

"Where were the Sahtu Dene from?" asked John.

"From the area all around Great Bear Lake," replied Etsi. "Their language is Slavey, but the two groups could understand each other."

"They would meet at the Johnny Hoe River each fall to make a huge fish trap together," continued Etseh. "The Sahtu Dene would start building the fish trap from one side of the

river and our people, the Dogrib, would start from the other side."

"Were they catching trout?" asked John.

"*Ile*," said Etseh. "Whitefish. It was a great time of working together and visiting. People celebrated with lots of food and tea dances that lasted for hours and hours. When the fishing was over, each group took dried fish back to their own area to be used in the winter."

Etsi got up and began dancing around the fire. "Come on, you three! Come and dance with me!"

Etsi and Etseh sang a tea dance song as they moved with rhythm in a circle. It wasn't long before Nora, Peter and John joined in.

"*Hotah!* Time to get packing," said Etseh, tired from the dancing. "The plane will be here soon."

"I can hear it!" called Nora from up on the hill.

Minutes later a blue and white Twin Otter circled the island and landed on the lake. The roar of the engines broke the friendly silence they had enjoyed for so many days. Opening the door of the plane, the co-pilot jumped onto one of the large floats, rope in hand.

Once the plane was shut down and tied to shore, everyone began grabbing gear and loading up.

"Kind of wet weather, eh?" said the co-pilot. Just as Peter was about to reply, down he went on the slippery rocks, right into the lake! Luckily he landed on his pack and wasn't hurt.

"Enough soakers for one trip!" he laughed.

"*Asanile*," smiled Etsi. "In a few hours you'll be home and into some dry shoes."

"In a few hours I'll be telling my parents all about this trip!" thought John.

Etseh was last to board the plane. He looked around one last time to make sure none of their gear was left behind. Then he took some tobacco out of his pouch and gently sprinkled it on the water.

"*Masi*," he said quietly. "*Masi cho!*"

The Dogrib people, or Tłįchǫ, as they refer to themselves, have traveled the Idaa Trail for centuries. They are part of the Dene Nation, which includes all the aboriginal people of the Northwest Territories who speak one of the Athapaskan languages. Archeologist Tom Andrews of the Prince of Wales Northern Heritage Centre in Yellowknife and his team, including Dogrib elders Harry Simpson and John B. Zoe, have been exploring the Idaa Trail and the relationship between people and the land for several years. They have produced an interactive website so that children can take a virtual journey of the trail, learning about sites of cultural and historical significance along the way. (See www.lessons fromtheland.ca.) This book is based on their discoveries and the elders' memories of traveling the trail when they were children. Here are a few additional notes on the sites in the story.

SHOTI LAKE

The remains of the two canoes found at Shoti Lake, and even the scarred birch tree, date back to 1939 when an early snowstorm forced Harry Simpson's family to continue their journey on the trail by dog sled.

VILLAGE BESIDE NIDZII

This village is the largest of four abandoned villages on the Idaa Trail. Traditionally, the Dogrib lived in caribou-skin lodges or spruce houses. But in the late 1800s, as the fur trade became more and more important, the Dogrib began to build log cabins with stone chimneys — homes that looked like the fur-trading posts which were increasingly a part of their world. In the treaty of 1921 mentioned in the story, the Canadian government secured land used by native peoples for "national interests," in this case, mineral development. There was little native representation in the treaty process.

The Sliding Hill and Blood Rock

Some say that there was a second slide at Sliding Hill where puppies were slid down the hill to see if they would become good sled dogs. Both of these sites are considered to be sacred because they are associated with Yamozhah, a mythic hero shared by many groups in the Dene Nation. There are many stories about Yamozhah, and he is known by a number of different names.

Komoola Portage

Portages offer the opportunity to rest, camp and tell stories, and for this reason they are important in Dogrib culture. The artifacts and remains found at old campsites also make them rich places for archeological study. In the past, the elderly men would lead the way over a portage, clearing the trail, while younger men and women followed with the canoes and supplies. Women used to carry the heaviest loads.

Hook Place

Fish, being more plentiful than either caribou or moose, were a major source of food. The Dogrib fished in summer and through the ice in winter. Depending on the location, they could catch lake whitefish, lake trout, pike, inconnu, loche, arctic grayling and walleye.

Grave Site

Grave sites and cemeteries are also sacred to the Dogrib people. Since the arrival of Christian missionaries, the Dogrib have buried their dead in graves marked by crosses and surrounded by white picket fences. Some say the fences are to keep the spirits from traveling. Before that, the Dogrib wrapped the bodies of their dead in clothing and left them to the elements, either on a burial platform or, in the barrenlands, on the ground.

Fence Narrows

Fences such as the one at Fence Narrows were built on lake ice in the spring to trap caribou migrating north to the barrenlands. The animals caught would provide food for the entire summer. In fall and winter,

Dogrib hunters would stalk the animals instead — they were easier to hunt at this time of year because they couldn't move quickly through deep snow.

HOTTAH LAKE

In a tea dance people form a large circle and sing as they move in a clockwise direction. The name "tea dance" may have come from fur-trading days when gifts of tea, ammunition and tobacco were sometimes given before the actual trading began. People would have a tea dance to celebrate the trading time.

Today the Dogrib have a population of about 3,000, and they occupy an area of nearly 390 000 square kilometers (156,000 square miles) between Great Slave and Great Bear Lakes in Canada's Northwest Territories. They recently signed the Tłıchǫ Land Claims and Self Government Agreement with the federal and territorial governments after nearly a decade of negotiations. The main goal of the agreement is to promote and protect the Dogrib heritage, culture and way of life.

NOTE

We have chosen to print transliterations for Dogrib words in the text, instead of printing them in the Dene font, to make the book accessible to young readers. These words appear in Dogrib in the glossary.

ACKNOWLEDGMENTS

The author and illustrator would like to thank Harry Simpson, John B. Zoe, Rosa Mantla, Lucy Lafferty, Philip Rabesca, Mark Heyck, Kyle Kelly, Gerri-Ann Donahue, the Prince of Wales Northern Heritage Centre, the Dogrib Community Services Board, the NWT Department of Education, Culture and Employment and, especially, Tom Andrews. If it were not for his research and dedication to this project, these stories would not have come to life in this book.

GLOSSARY

Transliteration	Dogrib	Pronunciation	Definition
Asanile	Esanìle	*(eh-sun-nee-lay)*	It's okay
Dawhidi	Dawhìdı	*(dow-hee-dee)*	Nothing
Dechi	Deechı̨	*(deh-chee)*	Fish cache on the ground
Dzon	Dzǫ	*(dzone)*	Here
Dzonchleh	dzǫ ı̨ı̨tłeh	*(dzone-clay)*	Come here
Etseh	Ehtsè	*(et-say)*	Grandpa
Etsi	Ehtsı̨	*(et-see)*	Grandma
He?e	Hę?ęh	*(heh-eh)*	Yes
Ho	Hoò	*(hoe)*	Let's go
Hotah	Hòt'a	*(hoe-tah)*	Okay
Ile	Ìle	*(eel-lay)*	No
Kligotse	Łıegotseè	*(klee-goe-tsay)*	Stickfish
Masi	Masi	*(mah-see)*	Thank you
Masi cho	Masi cho	*(mah-see-choe)*	Thank you very much
Nezi	Nezı̨	*(ne-zee)*	Good
Sah k'e	Sah ke	*(sah-kay)*	Bear tracks
Sehkw'on	Sęękw'ǫ̀h	*(say-kwoe)*	Listen to me
Ts'ekoa	Ts'ekoa	*(tse-koe-ah)*	Little girl

PRONUNCIATION GUIDE FOR PROPER NAMES

Dah?ak'e	Dah?ak'e *(dah-ah-kay)*	Nidziikaa	Nıdzı̨ka *(nind-see-kah*
Dogrib	*(dog-rib)*	Kogolaa	Kògòlaa *kone-go-lah)*
Gameti	Gamètı *(ga-may-tee)*	Sahtu Dene	*(sah-two den-ay)*
Hodoodzoo	Hodoòdzoo *(hoe-doe-dzo)*	Ts'idzoo	Ts'ıdzǫǫ *(tsee-dzo)*
Intse Ti	Ịts'èetì *(In-tse-tee)*	Tulita	Tulıt'a *(too-lee-tah)*
Idaa	Ịdaà *(een-dah)*	Whati	Whatì *(wha-tee)*
K'aawidaa	K'awıdaa *(kaw-wee-dah)*	Yamozhah	Yamǫ̀za *(yah-mone-zah)*
Komoola	Kòmǫòla *(kone-moe-lah)*		
Kugluktuk	Kugluktuk *(kug-luk-tuk)*		Tłıchǫ *(klee-cho)*
Kwajii	Kw'ajıı *(kwa-jee)*		The Dogrib people refer
Kwe?ehdoo	Kwe?ehdoò *(kweh-eh-doe)*		to themselves as Tłıchǫ
Kweikaa	Kwı̨̀ka *(kwee-kah)*